JUNIOR
CaEsaR

For Dave and his family, conquerors of Europe
C.I.

For Hope, Joe and Amandine – an inspirational triumvirate
D.W.

ORCHARD BOOKS
338 Euston Road, London NW1 3BH
Orchard Books Australia
Level 17/207 Kent Street, Sydney, NSW 2000

First published in 2013
First paperback publication in 2014

ISBN 978 1 40831 356 5 (hardback)
ISBN 978 1 40831 362 6 (paperback)

A CIP catalogue record for this book is available
from the British Library.

1 3 5 7 9 10 8 6 4 2 (hardback)
1 3 5 7 9 10 8 6 4 2 (paperback)

Printed in Great Britain

Orchard Books is a division of Hachette Children's Books,
an Hachette UK company.

www.hachette.co.uk

JUNIOR CAESAR

DAVE WOODS
CHRIS INNS

ORCHARD

We all know that Julius Caesar was Ancient Rome's greatest emperor. But before he became a mighty Caesar, he was, well…a mini Caesar.

Ergo, he was Junior Caesar!

There was once a great city called Ancient Rome.

And, in Ancient Rome, there was one particular place where people liked to *meet* and *greet*. And *walk* and *talk*. And *chit* and *chat*. And *umm* and *ahh*…

It was called the Forum.

(Not the Three-um or the Five-um, but the Forum.)

However, on this particular day in the Forum, people weren't just *meeting* and *greeting*. And *walking* and *talking*. And *chitting* and *chatting*. And *umming* and *ahhing*...

Nope.

On this day, the Ancient Romans were...

Roaming and *moaning!*

And what were these roaming, moaning Romans moaning about?

Their children!

"OUR KIDS ARE CRYING!" roared the crowd.

"THEY'RE PETRIFIED!" pleaded the parents.

"THEIR HOMEWORK'S TOO HARD!" groaned the gathering.

Some mini-mums were crying to the max.

And some maxi-mums were crying to the min.

Basically, they weren't happy.

History has it that amongst these moaning Romans there appeared a noble nipper – with laurel on his head (and hardy in his heart). One whose pencil was sharp and whose tongue was even sharper. With the wisdom of a senior, but the face of a junior…

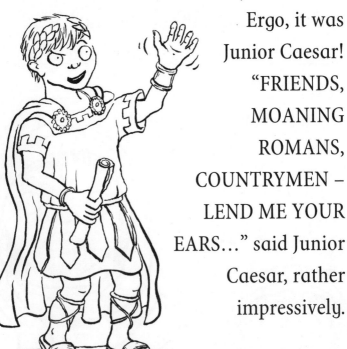

Ergo, it was Junior Caesar! "FRIENDS, MOANING ROMANS, COUNTRYMEN – LEND ME YOUR EARS…" said Junior Caesar, rather impressively.

The crowd looked Junior Caesar up and down.

(Well, mainly down.)

"Er, don't you mean LEND ME A BOX," remarked Rudus Remarkus, "to stand on?"

The throng tittered till their togas trembled.

"Or LEND ME A LADDER," smirked Sillius Twittus, "to climb up?"

11

The crowd laughed until their laurels lolled lopsided.

(They weren't short on height jokes.)
"YOU CHOOSE TO LAUGH WHILE YOUR CHILDREN CRY?" replied Junior Caesar. (That's the kind of big talk big people listen to… even from little people.)

The crowd's laughter was cut short.
(See.)

"LISTEN, CITIZENS OF ROME –
OUR TEACHERS ARE TOO
TOUGH."

Junior Caesar stood up to
his full shortness. "ARE YOU
FORUM OR AGAINST 'EM?"
he asked.

"AGAINST 'EM!"
cried the Forum.
"WELL, I'M
AGAINST 'EM,
TOO!" agreed
Junior Caesar.

The crowd were
beginning to like him.

(You could say he was growing on
them.)

"BUT, UNLIKE YOU, I SHALL RISE UP AGAINST THEM."

"What, like a soufflé?" said Gordus Ramsicus.

"NO, LIKE A SCHOOLBOY!" said Junior Caesar. "I SHALL EDUCATE THE TEACHERS! I SHALL USE THEIR LESSONS TO TEACH THEM A LESSON! I SHALL—"

"Er, we get the message," said the crowd. (Who were short on patience.)

"But how can you possibly win?" asked Doubtingus Thomus.

"Yes, you're just one person!" added Verius Scepticus.

(And if we're honest, Junior Caesar wasn't even one person – he was a half!)

"ERGO, I SHALL GATHER A MIGHTY ARMY TO FIGHT AT MY SIDE."

"An army of how many?" they asked.

"Dunno… Ten maybe?" replied Junior Caesar.

(Well, even great leaders have to start small.)

"And where will you keep your armies?" asked the crowd.

"Up my toga!" replied Junior Caesar.

And with that he nipped off to the playground to recruit his Legion of Little'uns.

JUNIOR CAESAR ⟶

"My Legion of Little'uns will be legends in their own lunchtimes."

⟸ **TOP-MARKS ANTHONY**

"Top in his class, top soldier and all-round top chap. (He's also my top friend!)"

SHORTUS SWORDUS ⟶

"Faster than a speeding swing. More powerful than a seesaw. Able to leap tall slides in a single bound. He's a super little fighter!"

"The all-action, pin-up girl of the Palatine Hill! She's got the right look – and a meaty right hook!"

⟸ **TITUS TROWSUS**

"Titus has high ambitions and an even higher voice. When he isn't singing falsettos – he's stuffing Cornettos!"

"Everyone thinks they're Smarticus. Top-Marks Anthony thinks he's Smarticus. I thought I was Smarticus…but no – apparently, *he's* Smarticus."

"Flashus is Ancient Rome's most famous rich kid. (And I've always liked the playground of the rich and famous!)"

ARCH E. TECTUS

"Arch put the (Roman) arch into architecture. He's built everything from aqueducts to aquariums – and even built the first (Roman) spectacles!"

FRUITICUS CAKE

"Mad about mixing fighting with cooking! Fruiticus invented some vicious dishes: Spear-ghetti, Lance-agne and to top it all... Bolus-nese sauce!"

LITTLE URN →

"Big urns are usually full of wines. It's the same with Little Urn – except he's full of whines!"

← **EDDIUS THE EAGLE**

"Beak of iron. Talons of steel. Heart of chicken. He soars high – especially when there's a battle going on."

TORTUS THE TORTOISE

"The most famous of all Roman tortoises. Tortus is a slow mover but a quick thinker, who runs on Shell!"

Junior Caesar gathered his Legion
of Little'uns outside the school
gates around 90 BC.

(That's 90 minutes
Before Cornflakes.)

"Our subjects are too
difficult!" moaned Little
Urn.

"WE MUST DIVIDE
AND CONQUER
THEM!" urged Junior
Caesar.

"But won't we get into trouble – you know, with the teachers?" quavered Titus Trowsus, nervously.

"IT'S POSSIBLE – ERGO, YOU MUST MAKE YOUR OWN CHOICE!" said Junior Caesar (quite bravely).

He walked straight through the gates into school…

"Ahead lies the battlefield," Junior Caesar declared.

The first lesson on the timetable involved…times tables.

(Worked out what it is yet?)

Yes, NUMERACY!

(And if you're scared of Maths – wait till you see the teacher.)

MISS ABACUS was an ogre (in a toga)…

who liked to create PROBLEMS…

by SUBTRACTING happiness…

and MULTIPLYING misery…

and ADDING heartache…

and DIVIDING friends…

She had no PLUSSES…

only MINUSES.

"SHUT UP!" shushed Miss Abacus.

(See.)

"Right, pupils," added Miss Abacus. "If 1 + 1 = 2. And 2 + 2 = 4. And 4 + 4 = 8. What is 8 + 8?"

"That's unfair, Miss," exclaimed Junior Caesar.

"Why?" said Miss Abacus.

"You answered the easy sums and left the hard one for us!"

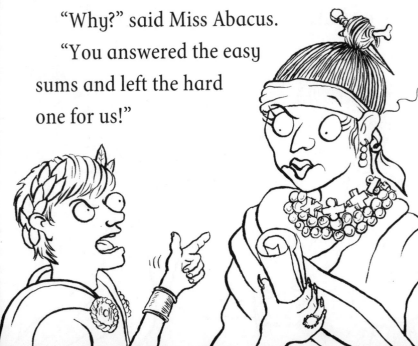

Miss Abacus suddenly SUBTRACTED her sense of humour. "VERY WELL, IF YOU WON'T ADD 8 + 8… WHAT IS HALF OF 8?

"Depends which way you cut it in half, Miss," answered Junior Caesar.

(Miss Abacus ADDED an angry shade of red to her cheeks.)

Junior continued. "If you halve it straight down the middle, it makes 3."

(Miss Abacus's anger MULTIPLIED.)

"And if you halve it across the middle, it leaves 0!"

Miss Abacus, who didn't like anyone to have a mind of their own, was suddenly MINUS anything to say...

Because Junior Caesar (whose mind was greater than the sum of its parts) had WORKED HER OUT!

Which was...A RESULT!

Geography was next on the timetable.

Today, their teacher, Grabbacus Thermos, was taking them to explore the Roman Empire.

They began travelling and soon passed a very tall island…

"Why's that mountain got hiccups?" asked Fruiticus Cake.

"That's Vesuvius," giggled Junior Caesar. "It's a volcano!"

(Titus Trowsus erupted in laughter.)

They kept travelling.

"We're now sliding through the slipperiest country in the world," said Junior Caesar.

"What's it called?" asked Flashus Cashus.

"Ergo, it is Greece!" grinned Junior.

They trawled through Gaul…where they almost got lost. But Lady Toga-ga found a well-travelled local called Sattus Navvus, who put them back on track.

Eventually, they reached Britannia
where, suddenly…
"THE MAP'S RUN OUT!"
exclaimed Junior Caesar.
He was right.
In front of the Legion of
Little'uns was…NOTHING!
No here…nor there.

No near…nor far.

Just a large dotted line stretching as far as the eye could see.

(Possibly even further.)

"LESSON'S OVER!" declared Grabbacus Thermos.

"You have now reached the limits of your little world."

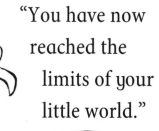

"But, Sir," pointed out Junior Caesar, "we can make our world so much bigger!"

"That's complete nonsense!" said Grabbacus Thermos.

"Actually," corrected Junior Caesar, "it's INCOMPLETE nonsense!"

(And he was completely right.)

Grabbacus Thermos (who knew his own limitations) stayed in his comfort zone looking very uncomfortable, because he realised…

Junior Caesar had broader horizons!

"Ergo, I shall expand The Known World!" said Junior Caesar.

And he did.

Just not on that particular day.

Because, as we know, Rome wasn't built in a day.

(And neither was the Empire.)

Once they'd marched back to school,
the Legion of Little'uns looked lively and
leapt to their latest lesson…
PUBLIC SPEAKING!
(That means being able to
talk clearly in front of friends…
and Romans…
and Countrymen.)

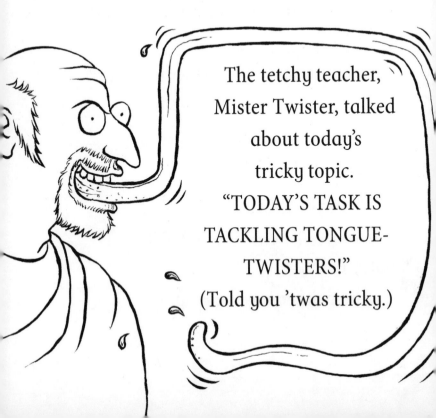

The tetchy teacher,
Mister Twister, talked
about today's
tricky topic.
"TODAY'S TASK IS
TACKLING TONGUE-
TWISTERS!"
(Told you 'twas tricky.)

"Repeat after me," insisted Mister Twister:

"MISTER TWISTER'S TONGUE-TWISTERS TEST TINY TONGUES…"

Twelve tiny tongues tried…but twelve tortured tongues…took a wrong turn!

Mister Twister smiled (a twisted smile) and said:

"That sentence you uttered
was utterly cluttered,
You muttered and stuttered
each word that you uttered."

"We'll try another," persisted Mister Twister.

Several school kids shifted slightly in their seats.

Seats that were covered in...?

(Yep, you guessed.)

RED LEATHER, YELLOW LEATHER, RED LEATHER, YELLOW LEATHER.

But before Mister Twister could twist again (like he did last summer), Junior Caesar seized his opportunity!

"MISTER TWISTER," he said. "DO YOU KNOW WHAT MY SISTER DOES?"

"No," replied Mister Twister. "What does she do?"

"SHE SELLS CENTURIONS' SHIELDS AT THE SHIELD STORE.
THE SHIELDS SHE SELLS ARE CENTURIONS' SHIELDS, I'M SURE."

"Can you repeat that please, Sir?" asked Junior.

Mister Twister was speechless.

"Mister Twister, I insist we try another…

MISTER TWISTER PICKED ON A PACK OF PRICKLY PUPILS.

DID MISTER TWISTER PICK ON A PACK OF PRICKLY PUPILS?

IF MISTER TWISTER PICKED ON A PACK OF PRICKLY PUPILS,

WHERE'S THE PACK OF PRICKLY PUPILS MISTER TWISTER PICKED ON?"

Mister Twister (who was well read) went even redder. The senior scholar stood and seethed…because Junior Caesar had seized the day!

Junior Caesar checked the timetable,
then led his Legion of Little'uns outside.

It was time for fun and (gladiatorial)
games.

Junior Caesar announced:

"THE NEXT CLASS IS STRATEGIC
MILITARY TACTICS AND COMBAT
MANOEUVRES!"

(Er…that's FIGHTING to you
and me.)

Now the problem was, the teacher
of STRATEGIC MILITARY TACTICS
AND COMBA— (sorry,
FIGHTING) was
called Couchus
Potatocus. And
he HATED
EXERCISE!

The only
thing he hated
more than exercise
was (surprise, surprise)
CHILDREN!

Today, he had arranged for Junior
Caesar and his Legion of Little'uns to
fight something especially colossal...
in the Coliseum.

(Go on, guess what it was...)

LIONS from Africa?
No.
ELEPHANTS from Asia?
Nope.
BULLS from Spain?
Nah.
Something worse?
'Fraid so.
It was…
DINOSAURS!
(Don't ask where
he got them from.)

"Your only chance," said a fierce young Ladiator (who was doing some even fiercer training nearby), "is to outwit them!"

"Maximus thankus!" said Junior Caesar.

And the DINOCATHLON began. (Which, by the way, is the oldest Olympic event.)

First, they had to play word scrabble against a STEPHEN-FRY-CERATOPS.

Which obviously spelt trouble.

But Smarticus Pants won hands down (and up and across) with his last word of the game:

E...X...T...I...N...C...T

And the X was on a triple-letter score!

Next came a sprint against a USAIN-BOLT-O-SAURUS (who was expected to win by a long neck).

But Junior Caesar showed why humans are ahead of dinosaurs – and ensured Shortus Swordus won…by starting a minute earlier!

"D'you-think-he-saw-us?" grinned Junior Caesar.

Finally, there was a big chariot race against the fastest dino-driver that ever existed.

The STIG-O-SAURUS!

The STIG-O-SAURUS was in a chariot behind a terribly quick (and terribly terrible) Tyrannosaurus Rex.

Against him was Junior Caesar in a small cart, which Couchus Potatocus had arranged to be pulled by Tortus the Tortoise!

(Yes, it was a slow coach.)

The race began…and things looked bad, until they approached a low bridge that had been built quickly by Arch E. Tectus…

Junior Caesar passed under the bridge with ease. But the Tyrannosaurus Rex – who should have (aqua)ducked – didn't…and became a Tyrannosaurus Wrecked!

The STIG-O-SAURUS was now
a STUCK-O-SAURUS.

The defeated Couchus Potatocus
boiled with rage at losing.

Junior Caesar looked up
towards his cheering Legion of
Little'uns in the Coliseum stands.
They were all giving Couchus
Potatocus the (biggus) thumbs
down…

"MASH HIM!" they cried.

But Junior Caesar
was merciful.

"I will spare
him," declared
Junior.

"Anyway,
he's had his
chips."

The next lesson was History. The History teacher, Quietus Pleasus, insisted every child be hushed up.

"Yours is not to reason why – yours is but to read and sigh," he told them, sternly.

But Junior Caesar knew that history would be…his story!

Finally, Junior Caesar and his highly organised Legion of Little'uns advanced upon their LITERACY lesson.

BUT THEY WERE SOON MET BY A HIGHLY DISORGANISED LEGION OF LETTERS!

The teacher, Genral Errorz, was preparing to engage them with words that weren't spelt correctly!

Today's subject was…**SPELLIGN!** (See!)

A WAR OF **WERDS** began!

Genral Errorz was writing wrongs. (And Junior Caesar was determined to right them.)

The Legion of Little'uns lined up against...The Armie off Mis-steaks! Junior Caesar rallied his troops: "Prepare your punctuation... Guard your grammar... Here they come!"

The Armie off Mis-steaks came marching towards them...

Wave after wave of badly spelt words...

First…

Soldeirs appeared – thousands of them!

But Junior Caesar wasn't afraid. He looked the soldeirs straight in the i…which should have been before e… (except after c).

"Erase on the count of three!" yelled Junior Caesar.

"1…2…3… RUB THEM OUT!"

Then Genral Errorz sent a group of
horse-drawn carts racing towards them!
They were…**charryots**!

"Sharpen your pencils!" shouted
Junior Caesar. "Rubbers at the ready!"

The Legion of Little'uns looked
a little spell-shocked…

But that was quickly erased. (As were the mistakes.)

Then a fierce, stripey **llger** came growling towards them.

"Remember to cross your *ts* and dot your *is*!" encouraged Junior Caesar.

(They followed him to the letter.)

And turned the llger…into a…tiger!

The SPELLING lesson finally finished – the last teacher had been taught a lesson.

"I stand corrected!" said General Errors.

(Which he was.)

And Junior Caesar was left in total command…of the language!

And so, his day's lessons complete, Junior Caesar returned to the Forum, where the roaming, moaning Romans…MOANED NO MORE!

"OUR KIDS ARE HAPPY!" laughed the crowd.

"THEY'RE DELIGHTED!" cheered the parents.

"THEIR HOMEWORK'S A DODDLE!" grinned the gathering.

"Veni, Vidi, Vici!" exclaimed Junior Caesar. Which, roughly translated, means: "I came, I saw, I conquered the curriculum!" (And if you've done your homework, you'll know what that means.)

It had been a mighty busy time for Junior Caesar.

"Ergo, I shall celebrate my triumph by taking an (early) ROMAN BATH!" he declared.

And off Junior Caesar went...to let off some steam.

And what became of Junior Caesar?
Well, that's another story…

DAVE WOODS
CHRIS INNS

All hardbacks priced at £8.99

Orchard Books are available from all good bookshops,
or can be ordered from our website: www.orchardbooks.co.uk,
or telephone 01235 827702, or fax 01235 827703.